THE REAL GHOSTBUSTERS

Ghostbuster
of the Year

Maureen Spurgeon

CARNIVAL

"Get moving, you guys!" yelled Peter Venkman. "There's a ghost on our tail!"

"The ghost we can handle!" Egon Spengler shouted back. "If only it wasn't driving a high-speed bus!"

"What d'you expect?" bawled Winston Zeddmore. "We're in a bus garage!"

"Dive out of the way, Ghostbusters!" Ray Stantz bellowed, glancing over his shoulder. "Here it comes!"

Horn blaring, engine revving, the bus smashed clean through the concrete fencing around the high-level parking bay, crashing down into the street below with a shuddering bang.

"Did you see that?" gasped Peter, almost before the dust had cleared. "It zipped through the rear window!"

"And it's heading back towards the garage!" Ray sounded quite indignant. "Any idea where it's going, Peter?"

"Just getting a Psycho-Kinetic-Energy reading!" Spengler announced, studying his PKE meter. "Yes – it's in the cafeteria!"

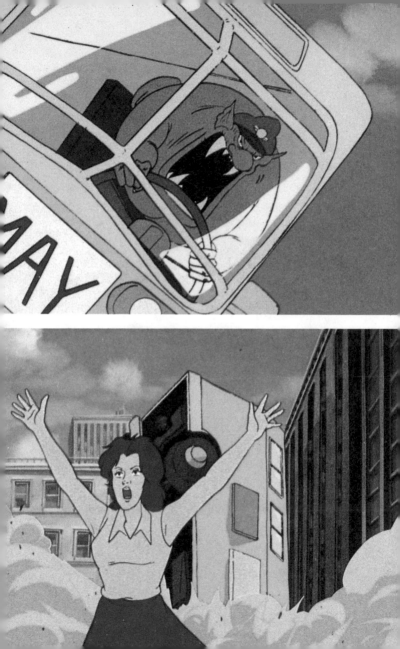

A whole row of passengers missed seeing the four Ghostbusters chasing a speedy spook – but it seemed they thought the game show on T.V. was a whole lot more exciting . . .

"He's slipped under the door of the men's room!" cried Ray. "Anyone got a coin to put in the slot?"

"Something quicker than that!" retorted Peter, quite enjoying the chase.

He raised his Proton Gun and blasted the door off its hinges, managing to duck just in time before the ghost flew out again, right over the heads of the Ghostbusters.

"There's only one bus left!" panted Egon, once they'd got their breath back. "I reckon that's where he's gone, now!"

"Okay," said Peter Venkman, very grim-faced. "So, let's go after him!"

Spengler's deduction proved to be correct — but the ghost wasn't giving up without a fight. He would have zoomed straight out through the door if plucky little Ray Stantz hadn't been right there with his Proton Gun. Then he hurled himself at the emergency exit, halted only by a stream of ion-beams from Winston. Egon Spengler was firing from the back door — so, in the end, all the ghost could do was to try and hide underneath a window.

"You're surrounded, pal!" yelled Venkman, taking aim from inside the bus. "Next time, leave the driving to us!"

Next minute, he was strolling out to face the waiting crowds, holding up his Ghost Trap in triumph, and greeted by a wild burst of cheering and applause. So many flashbulbs began popping all

around that the other three Ghostbusters had to shield their eyes.

"Doctor Venkman!" cried a cluster of newspaper reporters. "A few words, Doctor Venkman!"

Venkman handed over the Ghost Trap to Ray with a flourish. "Hold this for me, Ray!" he said grandly. "I think I'm about the meet the Mayor!"

"Tell us how you caught the ghost, Doctor Venkman."

"Well . . ." Venkman tried to look modest. "I did have some help from my assistants! They're great guys!"

"So----" One reporter whipped out a notepad. "You're Zantz, Stengler and Speddmore, that right? Tell us, what's it like, working with the great Peter Venkman?"

Luckily, before Stantz, Spengler or Zeddmore could think of a good reply, a tall, blond businesswoman edged her way through the crowds.

"Excuse me, Doctor Venkman!"

"You're not the Mayor!" Venkman was most disappointed.

"No." The dark eyes behind the designer-frame spectacles glinted coldly. "My name's Barbara Mantee, assistant to Mr. Charles Foster Hearse the Third!"

"Hey, Peter!" Spengler burst out. "That's the guy who publishes mags like 'Spooks Illustrated' and 'Boosweek'!"

"Right!" The woman gave a brief nod. "And Mr. Hearse has put me in charge of choosing this year's 'Spooks Illustrated' Ghost Hunter of the Year! Of course, the final decision has yet to be made . . ."

"But," she finished dramatically, "it will definitely be *one* of you! And Mr. Hearse would like to meet you personally before making up his mind."

The Ghostbusters could see that there was no arguing with this lady. Within minutes, they were being driven to meet the great Charles Foster Hearse, cruising along in an enormous, black limousine, wide enough to take up two lanes of the motorway!

Their destination was the famous Slime-Life Building, a towering, glass skyscraper with a lift that was large enough to take Barbara Mantee, plus the four Ghostbusters, and still leave plenty of room for a football team.

"I've brought The Ghostbusters to see you, Mr. Hearse!" Barbara announced, ushering them towards an enormous, ornamental desk, in the middle of an enormous, ornamental room.

"Good work, Miss Mantee!" murmured Mr. Hearse, and lowered the newspaper he had been reading, revealing a little, roly-poly sort of man, wearing glasses and fast losing his hair. "Thank you!"

Charles Hearse hauled himself on top of his desk

and held out a copy of the famous 'Spooks Illustrated' magazine, with a blank space instead of the usual cover photograph.

"Gentlemen," he said, "this is next month's 'Spooks Illustrated', the Ghost Hunter of the Year issue. The magazine was founded by my grandfather, the legendary Charles Foster Hearse. His portrait is right up there, on the wall!"

The Ghostbusters stared up at the forbidding face of a large, powerful man with a fierce moustache, brooding mouth and eyes which glared down at them.

"Wow . . ." breathed Venkman, with a glance at the man's chubby-faced grandson. "That's some millionaire publisher . . ."

"My grandfather's ghost still haunts Hearse Castle, the mansion he himself built!" Charles Hearse continued. "And The Ghost Hunter of the Year Award will go to the one man among you who succeeds in capturing it!"

"I'm sorry, sir," Winston Zeddmore said at last. "But none of us work on our own. We're a team — right, Ghostbusters?"

"Well . . ." Venkman considered, after a moment's thought. "Every team needs a star player----"

"I always read 'Spooks Illustrated'," Ray interrupted eagerly.

"And I've always dreamed about being on the cover!" Egon Spengler chimed in.

"Then," said Mr. Hearse, "you have until sunrise tomorrow for one of you to catch the ghost of Charles Foster Hearse!"

"And now," finished up Barbara Mantee, "we leave immediately for Hearse Castle!"

Hearse Castle turned out to be the most extraordinary place the Ghostbusters had ever seen. Turrets and towers, enormous domes and battlements, great, arched windows . . . The great Charles Foster Hearse had spared no expense.

Hearse Castle had its own scenery, too. Instead of the palm trees and orange groves which blossomed all around, the Ghostbusters found themselves being driven to the top of a snow-covered hill!

"Sorry it's only fake snow," Barbara Mantee apologised, "but Charles Foster Hearse always liked winter best."

Barbara Mantee was clearly used to taking all this in her stride.

"Here we are, Ghostbusters!" she said, unlocking a great, wide door and pushing it open. The gloom and foreboding of Hearse Castle seemed to come right out and hit them. "I'll return in the morning!"

"If you're still here," she added, as an afterthought.

"Wouldn't you guys like to think this over?" asked Winston.

"Every man for himself!" Peter announced, shrugging his thin shoulders.

"Do you know the Hearse library collection on the supernatural is the largest in the world?" Ray glowed with enthusiasm.

"I've always wanted to have a look around this place," Spengler chimed in, "ever since I saw it on the 'Haunts of the Rich and Famous' T.V. show!"

"Well, I won't have anything to do with it!" Winston declared stubbornly, folding his arms across his chest. "I'm staying right here until sunrise!"

"Suit yourself, Winston!" Peter called back, beginning to follow Ray and Egon. "See you later, maybe!"

The echoes of three separate doors being slammed shut resounded through the darkness for a long time. At first, Winston thought he was mistaken . . .

"Rosebud!" A deep, rumbling voice seemed to creep along the marble floor. "Rosebud . . ."

A huge pair of glowing eyes stared at Zeddmore from the shadows, blood-curdling chuckles floating through the darkening gloom . . .

"Maybe," Winston gulped, "maybe I'd better wait somewhere else!"

Meanwhile, Spengler was really enjoying himself in the Hearse Castle conservatory.

"Some of the finest specimens I've ever seen!" he murmured to himself. "Surely, this is a late-blooming nasturtium?"

"Rose-bud . . ." a deep voice answered him "R-o-o-ose-bud----"

"No!" persisted Spengler. "It's definitely a----"

How Spengler managed to reach his Proton Gun, he never knew. But next minute, the ion-beams were

streaking towards the ghost. There was an explosion, the sound of shattering glass – and Charles Foster Hearse had gone, Spengler's soot-blackened face looking around at the collection of smouldering, black sticks that had been exotic plants and flowers only moments before.

As for Ray Stantz, he was in the Hearse Library, happily gazing around at the vast collection of books which took up all of two storeys!

"Spirits of the Past . . ." he read in awe. "Ghosts I Have Known and Loved . . ."

"Rose-bud . . ." came a deep voice from the heart of the library. "R-o-o-ose-bud----"

Stantz held his breath and reached for his Proton Gun. "This is it!" he told himself, taking careful aim. "Ghost Hunter of the Year!"

No such luck! The ghost decided to disappear with a loud pop, seconds before the ion streams from Ray's gun reached their target. And as if that wasn't enough, all the books on the shelves began hurling themselves at Stantz, until he was being hit from all sides.

"Hey!" he yelled, raising an arm to defend himself. "Stop that, will you?"

There was a moment's pause. Then the whole library shook with the loudest thump anyone could ever imagine, the sound of every, single book being dumped in the very centre of the library, right on top of one unfortunate Ghostbuster.

"Aaaagh----!"

It was hard work, Ray discovered, fighting your way out from the heart of a solid book mountain – but he managed it at last, very bruised and battered.

"Ooooh---!" he winced, sucking his finger. "Trust me to cut myself on a bit of paper!"

And, Peter Venkman? He was thinking that the great Charles Foster Hearse had never been an animal lover, judging by the shooting trophies crammed along the entire wall of his vast Billiard Room. His every move was followed by two beady, staring eyes . . .

"Anybody home?" he called out, banging on the breast-plate of a suit of armour. There was no answer. "Well," said Venkman, looking around, "I guess this room's clean . . ."

"Of course," he added swiftly, as billiard balls began leaping out of the table pockets and whirling around in front of his astonished eyes, "I could be wrong!"

"Rose-bud . . ." wailed the ghostly voice of Charles Foster Hearse, amid a swirl of billiard balls. "R-o-o-ose-bud----"

Next minute, cue sticks began to glow, jumping off the rack and joining together like a giant matchstick man – a matchstick man heading straight for Peter Venkman.

"Sticking together, huh?" Venkman responded, getting ready to fire again. "I really admire tha-a-a-a-t----"

The last word became a yelp of surprise, Venkman toppling backwards on a stray billiard ball beneath his feet.

He knew he had to get out of the room. He slammed the door and leaned against it to hold it tight shut against the cue-stick man who was banging from inside until, one by one, the sticks rattled to the floor.

A storm was raging outside, he noticed, thunder crashing, and a jagged bolt of lightning flashing down on to a face which stared right at him, wild eyes gleaming.

Peter fired. But, the only reward he got was the sound of shattering glass, and pieces of broken mirror crunching under his feet.

"Blast!" he groaned. "There goes my image!"

There was a low, rumbling chuckle. At least, Venkman thought, the ghost enjoyed a good joke.

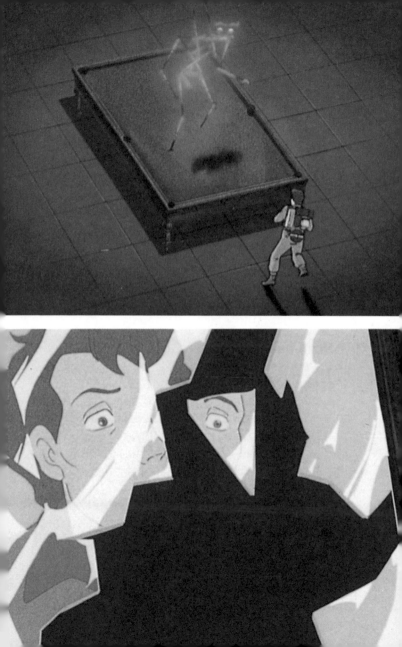

"Rose-bud!" the Hearse Ghost whined on. "R-o-o-ose-bud----!"

"Aaaagh! A-a-a-a-g-g-gh---!"

The whole mansion seemed to be torn apart by frightened yelps and terrified screams coming from the basement. Ion beams from three Proton Guns streaked through the darkness. Then there was a giant clap of thunder – and, by some strange chance, the lights came on.

"Oh, boy!" sighed Peter. "It's only you two!"

"Err – d'you come here often?" Ray asked, most politely.

"Hey!" Egon broke in. "Anyone seen Winston?"

There was a distant, piercing scream, the whizz of a Proton Gun being fired and the crash of unidentified flying objects falling to the ground.

"That sounds like him!" said Ray.

"Hang on, Winston!" yelled Egon, all three began to sprint past piles of crates, bits and pieces from Greek temples, whole pagodas, entire pyramids, statues, railway engines . . . A pair of legs in dark trousers was sticking out from under a heap of old furniture, bicycles, racks of clothes, pictures, vases . . . a whole pile of junk which had burst out of an enormous, shattered crate.

"Winston!" they yelled together, working like a conveyor belt, frantically trying to dig him out.

"This is all our fault!" groaned Stantz, grabbing an old child's sledge off the pile and thrusting it towards Spengler. "Ours, and that loony ghost who keeps wailing on about Rosebud!"

"How could we have been so mean?" cried Spengler, passing the sledge to Venkman.

"We should never have left him alone!" mourned Venkman, handing the sledge back to Winston Zeddmore, who was now safely brushing himself down.

"Hey!" protested Winston. He looked at the sledge more closely. "Know something? I had a sledge just like this when I was a kid . . ."

His words trailed away at the sound of sorrowful wails coming from the Hearse Ghost, floating towards them in a haze of light.

"Rose-bud . . . Oh, R-o-o-ose-bud----!"

"Okay, you guys!" whispered Ray Stantz. "This time, we've got him out-numbered!"

Four ion beams from four Proton Guns streaked towards the ghost.

"Great!" exclaimed Peter Venkman, grinning at the empty space where the Hearse Ghost had been.

The others could say nothing. Words seemed to choke in their throats at the sight of a giant statue glowing, coming to life, raising up to its full height with a low, threatening growl.

"Team work?" Peter was saying, blissfully unaware of the danger. "I love it!"

"Run, Peter!" Ray managed to cry out. "Run for it!"

"Follow me, you guys!" Winston Zeddmore shouted. "I found a way out of here! Aaaaagh! Who left that sledge lying around?"

It seemed the statue had also taken a fancy to the sledge, sweeping in towards the Ghostbusters with deep, thundering roars which deafened them all.

"Make for the door!" Winston commanded, carrying the sledge with him. "And be quick about it!"

"R-o-o-ose-bud----" the statue began to roar. "R-o-ose----" then it crashed into the wall and shattered into pieces.

And on the other side of that wall, the ghost of Charles Foster Hearse found that day was breaking, his glowing eyes gazed down at the snow-covered hill.

"Rose-bud . . ." he groaned. "Oh, R-o-o-ose-bud----"

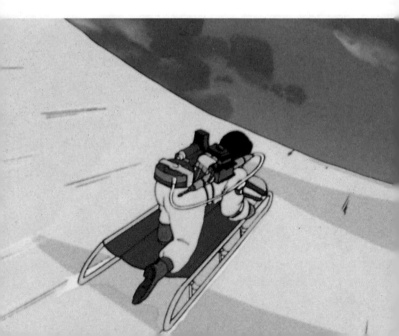

Winston Zeddmore liked the snow, too, and set the sledge down on the ground and hurled himself on top, ready to ride.

"Hey!" Peter shouted. "Why should you have all the fun? Come on, Ray and Egon!"

"Oooof!" (What else could Winston say with three Ghostbusters piled on top of him?) "Let's see if I can still manage this thing!"

"Gee, this is fun!" laughed Egon, as the sledge began shooting down the slope, gathering speed.

The Hearse Ghost didn't see why he should be left out of things. With another gruesome wail, he flew down the hill, beginning to roll into a giant snowball, until only the faint ghostly glow could be seen from deep inside. He was hot on the trail of the sledge, and the Ghostbusters.

As for Peter, Egon and Ray, they were enjoying their winter sports so much, they'd quite forgotten that Winston was still at the bottom of the pile, his face only inches away from the side of the sledge.

"Rosebud . . ." He read the name printed on the side. "Hey! D'you know what it says on this sledge?"

But, having three Ghostbusters riding on top, it was enough to make anyone's voice muffled.

"R-o-o-o-ose-bud----" came the familiar wails – from the glowing snowball, this time. "R-o-o-o-ose-bud----!"

"Yeah!" said Winston, trying to turn his head around. "It says Rosebud!"

Without any warning, the sledge went over a bump and flew into the air, throwing the Ghostbusters into a snow bank with such force that they almost vanished.

And still the sledge went on down the hill, with the ever-growing, ever-glowing snowball right after it, gathering speed the whole time.

"Get down!" screamed Venkman. "That thing's coming our way!"

But the snowball hit another bump in the hill, flying up into the air and over their heads, finally landing on the sledge with a loud SPLAT!

"Would you look at that?" demanded Venkman. "Can you see who I see, right there, in the middle of that snowball?"

"The ghost of Charles Foster Hearse!" Stantz and Zeddmore burst out, both together.

"And," added Spengler, "isn't he just having a whale of a time?"

"Rosebud!" whooped the Hearse Ghost in great glee. "Rosebud! Wheeee!"

There was one last swish of wooden runners over the snow, then the sledge and its ghostly passenger melted into the haze of a bright sunrise on the horizon.

"Would you believe that?" sighed Stantz. "He only wanted his old sledge back!"

"He liked winter best of all," Venkman reminded him. "And I guess there's a happy little kid in all of us!"

"Well," he added, seeing Barbara Mantee driving up in the Hearse limousine and looking every inch the stern business-woman, "most of us, anyway!"

"Did you catch the Hearse Ghost?" she demanded anxiously, clutching her clip-board.

"Which one of you did it?"

The answer came in a loud chorus, the Ghostbusters pointing at each other.

"He did!"

Everyone said it was the best-ever issue of "Spooks Illustrated", with a cover which opened out into a poster showing Egon Spengler, Peter Venkman, Ray Stantz and Winston Zeddmore, all looking very pleased with their title, "Ghost Hunter of the Year".

"Remember me saying you can get carried away by too much fuss and publicity, Venkman?" grinned Winston. "The main thing is doing your job well!"

"Sure," agreed Venkman. "You're always right, Winston!"

Carnival
An imprint of the Children's Division
of the Collins Publishing Group
8 Grafton Street, London W1X 3LA

Published by Carnival 1988
Reprinted 1989

ISBN 0 00 194437 1

Printed & bound in Great Britain by
PURNELL BOOK PRODUCTION LIMITED
A MEMBER OF BPCC plc